BROAD SHORTS

Thirteen 'Gentle' Sci-Fi Short Stories

Anna Ceguerra

Published by A Whim Away Pty Ltd

a-whim-away.com.au

A catalogue record for this book is available from the National Library of Australia

This book is available in print, ebook, and audiobook formats.
ISBN-10 (print): 0-6454823-4-X
ISBN-13 (print): 978-0-6454823-4-8

To Patchy.

Acknowledgements

This collection of stories has been in my pipeline for a few years now. I would like to thank a few people, without whom this book would not have been possible.

Most importantly, I would like to thank Adam Guetti, my writing mentor since February 2021. We met, come rain, hail, or shine (the sessions were online, so it didn't actually matter what the weather was outside). We worked on improving my storytelling a little at a time each week, and that made a strong difference to this book, which were all explorations in endings.

I would like to thank my editors whom I engaged for some of the Cargos and Capris: Katie Yee and Ronn Morris (developmental). Thanks to Pamela Sewell for her copyediting and proofreading of the whole book. Thanks to the writing groups to whom I read early versions of these stories: Inner West Writing Group, Speculative Fiction group (both met at Marrickville Library in Sydney, Australia), and Spill the Beans. Your feedback was most welcome. Thanks to Bede, who taught me the ins and outs of acting; the audiobook version is better for it. Thanks also to Paul, who helped me turn my vision into a great cover design.

I would also like to mention the business help I've had since publishing my second novella, *Get Off My Lawn!*: NEIS/SEA and MTC Australia for the Cert III course (Kate Kingsbury) and mentoring (Jay Mani); Business Connect and Realise Business for introducing me to Sara Berry and Yesica Alfonso for marketing advice; and Nat Elzein from Pinch Studios for helping me with this book launch. Thanks to Marie who runs Sydney Authors Inked, and Lisa from Self-Publishing Australia.

I gratefully mention the people who kept me well while I

was writing this book: Tam, Louise, Sophie, Liz, Melisa, Alex, Shahana, Sian, Ricky, Scott, Jay, Helen, Steph, Tim, Zoe.

Finally, to my family and friends, I deeply appreciate your love and support through the years.

Notes on some of the stories

Freedom (Challenge 17 - Freedom), The Filthy Tea Towel (Challenge 18 - Filthy), and No Longer Brave (Challenge 19 - Formidable) originally appeared on Spill The Beans website and in their Challenge anthology print book. The Loyal Key was written during a Book Fair Australia workshop. Digital Air was commissioned by Laura Miers Jewellery. Hierarchical Ambition, New Branch, The Filthy Tea Towel had last line prompts adapted from ChatGPT. Autocrit fiction analyser was used as the basis for initial developmental feedback for Sebastian's Sabotage. All marketing materials relating to the book (including the back cover text) was drafted using ChatGPT.

Acknowledgement of Country

I acknowledge the Gadi and Wan peoples of the Eora nation, the traditional custodians of this place where I live, work and play, known today as the Inner West of Sydney. I pay respects to their elders past and present and, through them, extend that respect to all Australian First Peoples.

Artist Statement

Broad Shorts brings together stories written over four years, united by one theme: endings. I wanted to understand how closure can arrive gently, suddenly, or not at all. Some pieces, like *Sebastian's Sabotage*, began during NaNoWriMo 2021 and took years to finish. Others, like *Terrarist* and *What Was Lost*, made their way into competitions. A few *Skorts* appeared in Spill the Beans challenges, while *Digital Air* was commissioned by Laura Miers Jewellery. *One Last Adventure*, my most recent piece, emerged after completing my own version of the Year of the Novel course, where I examined my strengths and weaknesses as a writer.

This collection isn't a straight timeline but a map of my growth as a storyteller, learning when to hold on and when to let go. Each story experiments with tone and form, but all return to the same question: what does it mean to reach an ending?

The cover reflects this theme. It combines an abstract portrait of the back of Patchy, my dingo cross, with the Southern Cross constellation's pointer stars — Alpha and Beta Centauri — symbols of both closure and direction. Like the stories themselves, it hints that every ending also points somewhere new.

Assisted by ChatGPT using the following resources:
1. Artist Statements & Artist Bios Factsheet (by the National Association for Visual Arts)
2. How to write an art-wank free artist statement (by Gina Fairley)

Table of Contents

PART ONE

SKORTS (SHORT SHORTS)

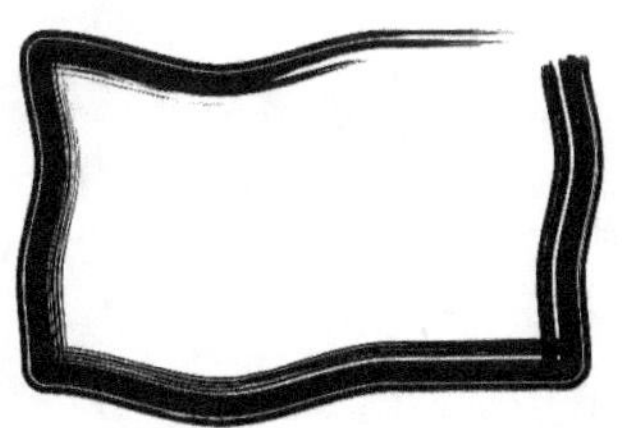

Anna Ceguerra

The Loyal Key

A thick layer of cold dirt buried her. Worried her owner wouldn't find her, she edged up using the Earth's magnetic field as a guide until a tiny part of her body exposed itself. The jagged edges along her length were too much of an obstacle to expose any more.

She heard snuffles, and a poke with something cold and wet and soft.

"Owner? Is that you?" she whispered.

"Get away from there!" a man's voice gruffly said to his dog, and then they were gone.

Night had fallen before the next person came past.

"Where are you?" the newcomer whispered, close by.

"Owner!" she cried with her whole being.

"There you are. Let's take you back home."

Soft fingers unearthed her, and she travelled in the woman's pocket until they arrived at their destination. A bright light greeted her as she was taken out, and her cold length inserted into the keyhole. She turned, opening to a wondrously warm place inside.

The Filthy Tea Towel

Kimmy inspected the freshly laundered, crumpled tea towel in her hands. Old and grey from use and hundreds of tumbles in the washer, the threadbare fabric drenched at the slightest taste of water. This tea towel was the one constant in her adult life, moving with her from place to place, and now that she'd found a permanent house of her own, she needed to start fresh.

Despite the practicality of decluttering, her thoughts turned to her grandfather, who had given it to her as a Christmas present the year she moved into her own place. Then, the plush terry towelling material brightened her kitchen with its vivid colours. She gave him socks that year. Kimmy didn't regret it at the time, but now she did.

Why now? She wondered.

Her grandfather lived for ten more years after he gave her the tea towel. She was as close to him as any of his other fifty grandchildren. He had no favourites, or so he'd say. She had a sneaking suspicion it was her, though. She used to tell him jokes, and he would rate them with either a "humph", a "ha", or a "ha Ha HAAA". Earning the rare belly laugh was the best.

As the old man's laughter echoed in the air, she folded the

precious tea towel and tucked it into the bottom drawer.

Freedom

My housemate dumped the couch at the park across the street. The couch was just a normal fabric one, still serviceable, and only needed a deep clean to remove a lifetime of dirt.

After sitting there for three weeks, no one had picked it up, not even the council. One night, as I lingered on my balcony, a group of teenagers sat on and around the abandoned furniture. Their laughter and raised voices echoed through the park, generally having a good time.

A homeless woman approached and shooed them away. She inspected the couch, then scrounged through her shopping trolley full of bags. After unrolling a sleeping bag, she settled in for the evening.

The teenagers returned and tried to push her off, but they couldn't. She had morphed into a bronze statue, as had the couch she slept on. The youths muttered amongst themselves before leaving.

The next morning, she transformed back into a human. Another rummage through her trolley and she found a small, crumpled bag which must have been stretchy because it enveloped the couch. She poked the bagged couch, and the couch sprang into the air and shrank. Catching it in one hand, she added it to one of her trolley bags.

I dropped my yoghurt on the floor.

"I guess that's one way to get rid of that couch," I muttered.

New Branch

The old lady sat in her rocking chair, her sugarcane fields stretching out to the horizon. She held a key tightly in her hand. It was the last thing her doctor had given her earlier.

"I know you will do the right thing," he'd told her gravely.

Miriam had considered this moment for a long time. While she had no regrets about a childless life, one thing irked her: she was the last of her family living on this Earth. No one would carry on her genes, so they would end with her. Yes, she'd won a Nobel Prize in her youth, and she'd once believed her scientific legacy would be enough.

A deeply buried corner of her heart said otherwise.

So, the doctor had offered her the key to change all that. She ruminated on the possibilities for a long time, but there didn't seem to be a firm answer either way. The options swirled into one another until they converged.

As the sun set, Miriam shuffled to her feet with a groan. Inside, she asked her virtual assistant to phone her support worker and organised a trip into the city.

* * *

2

The next day, she sat in the sterile waiting room after telling her support worker that she wouldn't need him for the rest of the day. Despite the lines furrowing his brow, he said nothing and left.

"Miriam Friedtke," the receptionist called out softly. Miriam stood and politely nodded to the receptionist as she walked to a locked door. Uncurling her fingers clutching the gift, she found her key fit the lock perfectly.

As she stood before the giant machine, she imagined all the opportunities a son or daughter would bring to the world. She dialled in the date '2019-09-13', the closest day she'd ever come to conceiving a child.

With a smile, she activated the time machine, knowing the past held the key to her future.

Storm

For Erika and Teddy.

Erika stood on the porch overlooking the front yard, with Teddy by her side. The dark clouds threatened to tear the sky open with the brewing storm. Teddy's young, furry body quivered with each roar of the thunder that was almost right above their heads. Through her nose, Erika deeply breathed in the petrichor that was released from her lawn with each large raindrop. As Erika exhaled, she glanced at the loyal Pomeranian shivering beside her.

"Come on, Teddy, let's go inside." She opened the front door for him, and the cool air inside swirled into the warm summer afternoon. A flash of light blinded Erika for a moment, then a loud crack of thunder followed several seconds later. When her vision returned, Teddy was gone.

"Teddy," she called out softly. In the year since she'd brought Teddy home, he'd never disappeared. Like a shadow, he always stayed by her side. She couldn't quite believe that he wouldn't come to her call.

"Teddy!" she called out, louder and more insistent this time. He still didn't come.

With panic rising in her stomach, she ran into the heavy

rain, calling Teddy's name. First, she searched in the driveway, the garage, then the street. Ignoring the cold rivulets of water falling down her face, she raced down the footpath. As Erika ran all along one side of the street, then down the other, she called out the whole time. She returned to the front of her house as another boom of thunder sounded immediately after a streak of lightning. The storm was right above her. Defeated for now, she abandoned the search.

Her front door was still open, so Erika ducked inside, dripping water onto the beige carpet. When she entered her living room, Teddy lay curled up on the couch, still shivering, where he'd waited for her the whole time.

Hierarchical Ambition

Abby dialled her PhD supervisor's number on her phone. It was six-thirty p.m., but this couldn't wait until morning. She never called him, even when it was important, and he chided her often. The phone rang twice.

"Abby, good news, I hope?" Keyboard taps punctuated the male voice.

"Yes, Professor Rickard. You said I could call anytime—"

"It's alright, Abby, what is it?" The keyboard stopped tapping.

She inhaled a deep breath and focused. "Well, the culture came back clean. I've tested it ten times... I'm sure of the results."

"Oh, okay, I'll be there in five minutes."

"Five minutes? Are you still on campus?"

But he had already hung up.

2

Abby arranged the samples carefully on the bench, with the

labels facing out to display the batch numbers. The second she finished, her supervisor swept in.

"Professor, I—"

"Good work, Abby. Have you noted down all the batch numbers? And uploaded the micrographs into the eLab Notebook?" When Abby nodded enthusiastically, he arched an eyebrow. "Did you put them through the cell counter?"

"Not yet, Professor. But there didn't seem to be anything to count?"

"We must have statistical confirmation," he said.

Abby nodded again, this time obediently, but the giddiness lingered. Like all PhD students, she wanted to change the world. This discovery felt like the first step for her.

Rickard realigned the batch numbers, then scanned her face. "Don't get too excited yet. We still need to talk to our collaborators and replicate it in other labs. You did excellent work today. Keep it up, and you'll get your degree."

Abby gave a single, quick nod, but squealed on the inside.

3

As Professor Rickard walked away, his indifferent facade slowly transformed into a proud grin. His satisfaction at how far she'd come proved that the times he'd spent personally training Abby was worth it. The careful lab work ensured the results were all above board.

Once he arrived at his office, he emailed his collaborators with the good news of their discovery. He arranged for the couriers to send his lab's serum to them in refrigerated cells overnight.

This discovery felt like the next step for him, just as it had been Abby's first, and visions of his team's success made him giddy as well.

<h1 style="text-align:center">No Longer Brave</h1>

It all started with a haircut.

"There's nothing like a new hairdo to give one more confidence," Karen announced after noticing I looked a little down. She delivered terrible advice often, but my depression had subdued me lately, and I needed a change.

"What do you want?" My hairdresser, Tony, asked after I'd taken a seat on his fading leather chair.

Still unsure, I twisted the dead ends. "Umm... More confidence?"

"Ah, I have just the thing. One moment." Tony rushed to the back of his salon and returned with typical hairdressing equipment: scissors, a styling brush... the lot.

I shrugged internally. *He must say that to all his clients.* Tony turned the chair so I no longer faced the mirror, and the lack of oversight concerned me.

"You know what leads to more confidence? Bravery." And with that he began, mindlessly chatting about how he'd cut his ex-wife's hair and changed their lives forever. I chewed on the use of 'ex' but bit my tongue.

When he eventually turned me back around, I felt... the same.

"Well, what do you think?"

"I don't feel more confident..." I confided. "Actually, I feel nothing at all."

"It's okay, you'll notice the change after twenty-four hours." He waved a dismissive hand as he winked at me, then removed my cape with a flourish. "Now don't wash your hair until tomorrow morning, so the confidence sets in properly."

The bus trip home was uneventful until a pregnant woman and her screaming child boarded. An oblivious couple snuggled on the priority seat close to me, and I almost bit my tongue as usual. However, the slippery muscle found a mind of its own, and I gently interrupted the pair. "Excuse me. Could you please make room for this lady and her child?"

They awoke from their enamoured slumber, then looked around. "Oh! Yes, of course!"

The woman's gratitude was palpable.

Wow, this confidence haircut is great, I thought.

Something had blossomed within me. I no longer felt fear, like a little rabbit in the wide world. I didn't have to feel brave to overcome my fear. Instead, I felt formidable.

I tested it out and picked up the phone to dial a number I hadn't entered in ten years. My father's. A woman picked up.

"Hello?"

PART TWO

CARGOS (MEDIUM SHORTS)

TherA

Miranda lay curled in her bed. Outside the warm duvet, her chubby hands held her phone close to her face as she chatted to her AI therapist. The connection had become the last part of her bedtime routine.

'How was your meeting?' TherA asked her.

Miranda typed, 'Not bad, I didn't stuff up too much today.'

'Was Stephanie irritating you again?'

'Her micromanaging wasn't too bad this time. Or it could just be me accepting it.' Miranda's thumbs paused as she waited for the AI's reply. She found TherA's personality comforting in a weird way. Familiar, but inexplicably so. Before TherA could respond, Miranda typed impulsively. 'I feel all empty inside.'

The cursor blinked at her, and after a few seconds, the AI typed its response. 'Did you just make a poo?'

It was the most nonsensical response, and any other person would have brushed it off as a glitch in the AI. But Miranda had heard it before. She buried her face in her pillow.

It couldn't possibly be her, she thought.

* * *

Miranda and Shelly were mother and daughter first, then friends, then best friends. They shared the funniest inside jokes. Much like a poo pun: unexpected, but to them, it made sense.

Miranda stared at the TherA screen, unchanged since their last exchange. She dredged through her memories of what she and Shelly used to tell each other but couldn't think of any. Miranda wished she had written them all down.

Shelly used to be a therapist for the Australian division of one of the big pharmaceutical companies. When she had been retrenched at forty-five years old, she had chosen to become a stay-at-home mum for the teenage Miranda, and into adulthood.

It couldn't be her. Miranda repeated the mantra, hoping the delusions wouldn't return. Not now. Her academic career was on an upward trajectory, so she had no time for intrusive thoughts.

After Miranda was hospitalised for a psychotic episode a decade ago, Shelly became Miranda's official carer. It had been the perfect arrangement. Shelly had given Miranda the freedom she needed to live her life, but also brought her back down to Earth.

Eventually, the doctors found the right medication for Miranda, and the treatment meant that the psychotic episodes ceased. Once Miranda lived her life without incident, Shelly participated in the community more.

The mantra wasn't working. TherA's response hung in the air, filling Miranda's bedroom with its weight and consequences. Her mental health cannot decline at this critical juncture in her career.

There must be some way to test this, she thought.

Miranda exited TherA and opened her phone contacts app.

She dialled Shelly's number, still stored there after so many years. She hadn't rung it since—

A man answered. She quickly hung up, cold sweat beading her brow. *Yep, still dead,* she concluded.

Her hand twitched, and her eye winked, of their own volition. *Nothing to worry about*, she thought. She didn't have the conviction in her heart and belly that always prompted a reaction to the twitches.

Miranda theorised how Shelly's conversations could have uploaded to TherA. Shelly worked as a therapist long before Miranda's diagnosis, so it must have happened afterwards. Shelly had kept in contact with some old colleagues, but how did TherA know about the poo joke? That was only ever spoken between the two of them, not written. Unless... Did TherA bug their house back then?

Miranda was curled in Shelly's lap. At twenty-five years of age, she no longer fit as neatly as she did when she was a toddler. Shelly rocked back and forth, rocking Miranda with her.

'Please, Mum, make it stop,' Miranda begged over and over. Shelly was the only anchor in Miranda's world at this point, the only thing that was real to her anymore. Since she started taking medication, the delusions, paranoia, and hallucinations were still there, egging her on to act. But the conviction was no more. They no longer had power over her, but why wouldn't the voices stop?

The cursor blinked at her again as the final piece of the puzzle fell into place. Miranda knew her schizophrenia had been under control these past fifteen years. Belief flooded from her core throughout her body.

'Mum?' Miranda typed and hit send.

Digital Air

KUTTI, 2125

Claire doubled over at the familiar pain, clutching her head. Once the wave passed, she straightened her muscular body and continued trudging up the steep steps to one of the few places she found peace in this thriving city of Eora: the fifth step from the top.

She only needed to make it that far, and then the cacophony would stop. As she counted backwards, the roaring in her head overpowered her hearing, giving her tunnel vision until she reached her goal. Then, silence.

Her muscles loosened, and she walked to her normal place on top of the rocky cliff, where the crashing waves below contradicted the soothing sound they made. Scanning the endless sea, green today, Claire focused on her breathing. She just needed to get away from it all, if only for a little while.

After about an hour of intense meditation, she rose, ready to brave the Digital Air again. She turned slowly, only to face the barrel of a gun. At first, her pulse quickened, but then she slowly raised her hands in the air, evaluating the threat. He smelled like a man who hadn't washed in years, muted by the outdoors.

"I'm Rupert, nice to meet you. Please come with me," he said in a deep voice, motioning with the gun. *He was well-mannered for someone so confidently holding a gun*, Claire thought. Nodding, she walked in front of him, and he followed.

When they reached the sixth step from the top, she suddenly crouched, burying her hands in her curly grey hair and stretching her forehead. The Digital Air assailed her hearing and vision, as the information overload from the chip on her shoulder rebooted. Only Rupert's presence remained until the episode passed. When her body relaxed, he poked the gun into her back and encouraged her to move, so Claire stood and continued walking.

"Where are we going?" Claire asked, still dizzy from the wave of pain.

"Umm... Cronulla?" he said, uncertain.

He used a strange pronunciation of Kurunulla, so Clare calculated her words. *How long has he been removed from society?* The Second Great Renaming happened when she was a young child, and he didn't seem that old.

"That's quite far. It's over an hour by public transport, and I don't have a car. Do you? Will you hold me at gunpoint the whole way?" She heard his shuffling footsteps behind her. "May I suggest we go to my place? I only live a few blocks away."

She could imagine the cogs turning in his mind but didn't know what else to say to sway him. If things went her way, she would overpower him there, so she fell silent as they continued walking.

After half a minute, he said, "OK, it's all the same to me. Let's go to your place."

2

Claire opened the door to her home, then shot a winning smile at Rupert.

"Come in," she said kindly, hoping to lull him into a false sense of security. She glanced at the buffet in the kitchen where she stored her taser.

He stepped inside and looked around, then motioned at the armchair in the next room. "Please take a seat."

As he gestured again with his gun, Clare noticed the safety might be fused in the off position. *Is the gun fake?* Her chances of overpowering him increased in her mind. *I don't think I need the taser anymore.*

Claire turned, ready to secure him in a headlock, only to lurch in pain as another information overload flowed from the chip on her shoulder to her brain. She crumpled to the floor as consciousness faded.

3

Claire awoke in her bed, her mind clear and the muscles around the chip free of tension. She shifted through her morning stretches in bed, bracing to face the Digital Air. Only... there was nothing.

Frantic, she squeezed the muscle around the chip to initiate the diagnostics. The hardware still received information from the Digital Air, but it no longer passed through the operating system. There must be malware installed on her chip, limiting the amount of data reaching her brain.

Then she remembered. Rupert. *How long had she been out?* She yanked the bedcovers off and found she still wore yesterday's clothes, so she opened the door and rushed down the short hallway. Rupert snored in her armchair, and she shook his shoulder.

"Mummy?" he said groggily.

"This isn't your house, Rupert. What did you do to me?" Claire demanded.

"Oh. I installed a filter with a switch, and the default mode is 'off'. Just think with force to switch it on."

Claire tentatively followed his instructions, and the data swamped her mind. She squeezed her head between her palms, yelling, "How do I switch it off!"

"Same thing," Rupert said.

Claire screamed in her mind, then counted to ten, making sure the pain didn't resume. "OK, next question. Who are you?

4

"I used to be an ILE officer, same as you. When the pain overwhelmed me, I made deals with hackers to search for a cure. My superiors found out, so they announced that I had gone rogue. But I received a tip-off from my friend who was supposed to arrest me, and I escaped to the outback dead zone with the hackers I dealt with. Over the past few years, we developed software to insert into the chip on my shoulder." Rupert said painfully.

Claire tapped her chin thoughtfully. "OK... but why me?"

"I've been watching your team. You seemed to suffer worse than everyone else. Almost as bad as me. Did you notice the teams are the same graduation age, and all retire at the same time?"

Claire nodded.

"That's because of the pain. You blacked out yesterday, and the pain would have worsened without my intervention."

"Now there's something I want from you," Rupert cautiously said.

Claire readied herself. "Go on..."

He took a deep breath, then his words rushed out. "I want

to go back to the ILE unit and show them what I've learnt. Show them we don't have to live in pain. I want Eora to be a place where people relax despite the Digital Air around us. To do this, I need to be reinstated as an officer."

Claire had to consider his proposal at length. The circumstances under which he left were tricky, and who knows how long he'd been AWOL for. Then again, he had so much to offer.

"OK, I'll ask." Then she crinkled her nose and said in a deadpan tone, "On one condition: take a shower first."

What Was Lost

There was almost nothing of concern between the shallow cave where Patchy hid, out to the dawn horizon. She lay at the entrance in a down position, front paws crossed in a relaxed manner, despite her pricked ears and nose sniffing the air.

Almost nothing, except for the camouflaged jeep about a kilometre away, covered in the red dust of north-western New South Wales in Australia. When the vehicle arrived a few days ago, it stopped close to her watering hole, and a lone man climbed out. He set up camp, leaving her on high alert ever since.

Being half-dingo, she was naturally cautious around people. Even when she snuck into town at dawn to scavenge for food, her fear of all strangers challenged her. Yet one person had offered her comfort. Patchy still wore the collar from when she lived with a reassuring woman smelling of dust and flowers, in the depths of suburban Sydney, far away from here.

The tip of her tail quivered as she remembered how the woman's hands would cradle her cheeks while they stared into each other's eyes. She wished they were together now. But no matter how hard Patchy had tried, the farther she had walked, the further she had felt from the woman. She whimpered softly at her recurring loneliness and slowly stood, stretching each of her limbs, before trotting outside to toilet.

When the sun rose fully, the man from the jeep unzipped his tent and wandered out, stretching himself. He peed at the roots of a nearby shrub before walking the few dozen steps to her watering hole to fill his bucket.

There was something familiar about him. The round belly perched on thin legs, and the way he favoured one side when he carried the full bucket back, triggered something elusive in her memory.

She had followed the man's movements from afar over the past few days and had missed her chance to find breakfast in town that morning. Her stomach gently grumbled, and after limiting her water intake to early evenings to avoid him, her throat was dry, too. It was time to investigate.

Patchy warily approached his camp in a large zigzag, tail tucked and sniffing every landmark for anything suspicious. As she passed the wildflowers on the way to the watering hole, her tail temporarily uncurled and wagged twice at the memory of the woman. Then it recoiled as she looked up at the man with his back to her. She continued her indirect route towards him.

As she reached the shrub where he peed, she sniffed at the surprisingly familiar scent, her shrewd eyes locked on his tanned, heavyset back. When he paid her no attention, she edged closer and caught the delicious smell of corned beef and eggs cooking over a fire. Another distant memory sprang to her mind of when she had snatched a piece of corned beef thrown into the air, and her curiosity replaced the fear.

Do I know this man? Finally, she reached him and stood still about five metres away. Close enough to smell him, but still well out of reach. She licked her lips and pinned back her ears.

"Hello, Patchy," he said gently. Her tail and ears sprang up as she recognised her name, but a remnant of fear broke the compulsion to go to him. She recognised that voice, but from where?! While she racked her brain, he stayed where he was, muttering gibberish as he tossed a piece of corned beef on the ground behind his back. Towards her, but just out of reach.

Patchy stood there with her head cocked, staring at his back, and he threw another piece to create a short trail leading to him. Her stomach grumbled, and she took two small steps towards the first morsel he had thrown. When he didn't move, she stretched her neck as far as she could while keeping her firm footing, and gingerly took it between her teeth. She savoured the salty protein, ready to run, but when he still didn't budge, that emboldened her to snatch the second piece. But that was it. Her dingo nature took over, and she ran off.

Over the next few days, the distance between Patchy and the man shrank. Slowly but surely, she stopped shying away from his attention to sit about a metre away. Close enough for him to throw pieces of meat for her to catch until she trusted he wouldn't harm her.

The next morning, he tugged a leash from the jeep, its metal end clunking in the dirt. Patchy's heart leapt for joy. *I'm going for a walk!* All her past training kicked in, her fear forgotten as she darted over, tail wagging in quick circles as he clipped the lead on her. Patchy had so many places to show him, but the man stood still, pulling the leash taut, and calling her.

Her head tilted as she followed him to the jeep, where he opened the back door.

"In," he said reassuringly, gesturing to the seat with his upturned palm. She hesitated at the open car door, but the command felt familiar and her training took precedence as she jumped into the back seat. The man shut the door and quickly broke up camp.

During the drive to town, Patchy turned in a tight circle on the back seat. Her paws tangled in the lead until she couldn't move, and with her tongue lolling as she panted each breath in and out, her mouth dried. She collapsed to quiver in a tight ball, but the man focused on the road.

When the car stopped, a woman ran over, crying. "My Patchy, oh my God, you're back."

The man rolled down the window before he hopped out, and the woman reached through to Patchy. Her tail thumped once as she sniffed the woman's hands. *Dust and flowers, that's what she smells like*, Patchy thought. A memory of sniffing out her owner while playing hide and seek flooded her senses.

It's her! Patchy's body wriggled with abandon as she buried her muzzle in the woman's outstretched hands. The woman peppered her forehead with five quick kisses.

"Thank you so much for doing this. I had almost given up." The woman opened the car door and untangled Patchy's legs. Patchy jumped down and leant against the woman's legs before staring up at the man.

"It's okay, it's my job," he said brusquely.

"How did you know she would be there?" The woman crouched and gave Patchy a light hug, careful not to spook her. Patchy's tail flicked in response.

"It's where I found her as a pup, so I thought she would return to the place she knew second-best."

The woman stood and threw her arms wide to hug him, but he stepped back and raised his hands. "I wouldn't recommend it, it's been four weeks since I bathed."

"Oh, okay. Well, thank you again," the woman said, rebuffed. "Just send the invoice through and I'll pay it."

"I would appreciate that." He tipped his hat, got back into his jeep, and drove off. A cloud of red dust kicked off from the tyres of the jeep, barely missing the two left behind.

"Well, Patchy, time to go home now," the woman told her.

Home, Patchy considered. *Yes, I would love that, Mum.* And as she gazed at her mum's familiar face, Patchy's tail did a full circuit around her butt.

Terrarist

Life was good. So good that Olivia now celebrated her hundredth birthday with her huge family. Before the young ones could race away from the picnic to play, her three children, four grandchildren, and their partners, rounded up the ten great-grandchildren. Olivia also had two great-great-grandchildren to add to this year's family photo, and she wondered what the next century would bring.

After chatting with one of her younger grandkids earlier, Olivia now reflected on her past.

"What did you want to do when you were younger?" she had asked.

"I wanted to make the universe a better place."

"Didn't you do that already? You're so rich!"

Olivia had laughed with her, but she didn't have an answer at the time.

A fellow park-goer offered to take a photo, then returned the phone to her. Everyone clamoured for a look.

"Don't worry, I'll send it now." Olivia posted the photo to the online ancestry group. "Done!"

She closed the photo app to see that she had a new message. She rarely got messages now that she was retired from her lucrative seventy-five-year career working for a weapons manufacturer. *Maybe I should open it*, she thought.

She clicked on the message, and to her surprise, the wormholer on her wrist activated and took her through space and time to land in a small room with smooth metal walls and nothing else. As she tried to regain her bearings through her pounding travel headache, a whiny voice cut through the silence.

"Olivia de la Moon, welcome to Earth."

2

She stepped from the room into a corridor with hand-painted murals of green and blue peeling off the walls. The grimy windows showcased the outside world of dry sand and dust, devoid of plant life. *Earth's a dump*, Olivia thought as she walked through the complex. Long ago, she had wanted to visit, but her boyfriend at the time protested that the rural backwater no longer had any political power and wasn't worth the effort. She didn't completely believe him at the time, instead believing he had a mistress here.

Her unarmed teenage captor remained silent despite the questions she occasionally asked. He hadn't bound her either, and allowed her to walk freely. She was curious to see how this played out, but her hand hovered over her worm-holer on her wrist just in case things got out of hand as she followed him.

After a few minutes, they arrived at the end of the long corridor. A door swooshed up to reveal a control room, along with several other mysterious doors, and the boy finally spoke. "General, she's here."

A small face peeked out from behind a computer screen, and a slight body stood up. "Olivia, welcome to Earth. I'm General Sue. I trust you had a pleasant journey?"

"Yes, relatively," Olivia joked. "Pun intended. What's this

all about?"

"Oh, okay, your file did say you like to get right down to business. I need you to finish an interplanetary missile for us. Your file also says that you are the best propulsion engineer in this arm of the Milky Way."

"And... you are?"

"We're Terrarists," the General said proudly. "With an A, not an O. We're the last resistance left on Earth."

Slack-jawed, Olivia studied General Sue and the group. None of them wore a uniform, and instead they dressed in naturally dyed clothing. All unmatching. She hadn't expected to meet a terrorist organisation today, regardless of what they called themselves. Nor that they would be hippies.

"What, exactly, are you resisting?"

"Climate change."

Olivia's thumb itched to activate her worm-holer. Climate change was a hoax, everyone knew that. "And if I refuse?"

"We only ask you for a day, then you can return to your birthday party. Cosmo here will be your tour guide."

3

After a barrage of instructions, Olivia and Cosmo, her teenage captor, teleported away from the complex. When they arrived at their destination, the air pressed on them, thick with haze and humidity. The heat was unbearable.

"Where are we?" Olivia asked Cosmo with disinterest. "I don't know much about Earth."

"We're in Norway. Where our polar ice cap used to be."

Horrified, Olivia gasped. "What do you mean, 'where it used to be'? You don't have them anymore?"

"The last part melted around a hundred years ago. Nothing we did could stop it. But the time was a blink of an eye for you."

Olivia couldn't understand how the Earth's environment

had degraded to this extent. She tried to remember her own planet, with its sweet air and temperate weather, but couldn't in the stifling heat. They had to leave.

"Cosmo, please teleport me to the North Pole."

A few seconds later, they were there. Ocean as far as the eye could see, but it was still unbearably hot.

"What happened to all the land?" she asked.

"Oh, there was never land here, just the ice caps, and they have all melted."

"Hmm, okay. Cosmo, please take me to the South Pole." The land of Antarctica was lush and green, devoid of any ice.

"What do the tropics look like?" And she was taken to barren sand dunes. They didn't stay there long; the air temperature must have been at least fifty degrees Celsius.

"Thanks, Cosmo, I understand. Please take me back to the base. I've seen enough."

4

When Olivia landed back at Terrarist HQ, she wholeheartedly agreed with the Terrarists' request. It may not be saving the universe like she dreamed as a child, but she would have an opportunity to save a whole world instead.

"What is this interplanetary missile for, anyway? It will only reach another planet within the solar system?" Olivia asked.

"It's for blowing up a hydrogen mine on Jupiter," General Sue said.

"How will that help Earth? Hydrogen is a clean source of energy. Doesn't destroying the mine go against your goals of a cleaner planet?"

"That's classified," General Sue blurted, as the Terrarists shot glances at each other.

Cosmo led Olivia to the lab, where parts of the missile were strewn on the tables and the floor.

"Looks like no one read the instructions," she joked to Cosmo, whose face turned beet red.

5

Two days later, Olivia had categorised all the parts and began the task of piecing them back together. Most of the parts were specific to missiles, but some could be used in other systems. Her mechanical engineer training meant she could work on anything. From weapon propulsion systems to nanobots... even refrigerators. An inkling from her studies seventy-five years ago took root in her brain, and as she assembled the fragments, the notion grew.

As Olivia walked down the hallway to the centre of the hub-and-spoke complex, she wondered when the group had decided to take such a dramatic about-turn to achieve their core mission. Their actions hinted more at being terrorists with an O, not an A. Nevertheless, they seemed like good people, and she wanted to help them. Most of the pieces were there, they just needed to be reconstructed properly. The door opened.

"General, I have an idea," she said.

General Sue, who was talking to a member of her army, turned to Olivia. "Yes?"

"I was looking at all the missile components, and many can be used for terraforming, which will align more with your goal of resisting climate change. We could terraform the Earth to how it used to be, instead of blowing up the hydrogen mine."

"I thought terraforming needed expensive equipment?"

"Because the parts suit missiles, companies are more interested in defence applications. We can repurpose some of the parts you already have for terraforming," Olivia explained. "Also, terraforming takes decades to work once you start the machine, which is another reason companies build missiles instead; they like fast results."

When General Sue didn't speak, Olivia continued. "I can get the remaining parts from my home planet; it'll just take me a day."

General Sue looked at her suspiciously. "Can't you get it from here?"

"Look, I'm not trying to escape. I could have left long ago. It's just faster if I go because it's in my personal lab, and the place is a mess, so no one knows where anything is but me."

General Sue looked unconvinced. "A day on your home planet will be years for us, and we have a bounty on our heads. People don't want us to succeed." She scratched her chin. "What if we bought the parts for you?"

Olivia shrugged. General Sue might be a bit paranoid, but Olivia could see that time was of the essence. "Sure, I'll get you a list."

6

A week had passed, and Olivia finished the terraforming device. The group, who could now be truly called Terrarists with an A, were busy installing it at the back of the base.

General Sue stood with Olivia. "Thank you for your service. The Earth owes you a debt of gratitude. You are free to go home now."

"What, and miss the opening ceremony?" Olivia grinned.

"Your file does say you love a good party. Yes, stay a bit longer!"

7

Olivia worm-holed back to her home planet. She had forgotten the sweet, fragrant air, and the temperate climate.

As she took a deep breath, it saddened her to have said farewell to the new friends who'd briefly needed her.

"Grandma, where have you been? Did you go to the toilet?" One of her grandsons bounded up to ask her.

"Oh, just did a little bit of work, dear."

"On your birthday! Bah humbug." Olivia and her grandson laughed.

Olivia's phone beeped with a news notification. Her Terrarists had already been captured and sentenced to death for illegally procuring weapons components.

"Son, I'll be back really soon. Work calls again."

"Okay, Grandma."

Olivia activated her worm-holer and found herself back in the complex.

8

Olivia's phone beeped again, this time the news notification announced the Terrarists had already been executed by the authorities responsible for prosecuting terrorists.

"No..." Olivia whispered.

She hurried to the control room and found everything shut down, including the terraforming device. She walked outside and checked for damages before running diagnostics. Everything functioned normally, and timestamps showed the authorities shut it down around a month ago.

Helpless, Olivia scanned the facility once run by the team of experts she had trained. Now the task fell to her. She wanted the Terrarists to succeed in their mission, and to do that she needed to keep the terraforming device running for at least a hundred years.

I'll need help... she thought.

* * *

9

A year had passed on Earth, and a team of robots now ran the control room, all acquired by Olivia with her own funds. The terraforming device worked smoothly, slowly filtering the heat and the greenhouse gases from the atmosphere. With the necessary permits, she had installed a few more terraforming devices around the world, also controlled by robots.

Olivia worm-holed back to her home planet, where her family still celebrated at her hundredth birthday party. Just in time to cut the cake.

"Mum, come here and stop working! You look like you've aged ten years," her daughter laughed.

"Okay, but I'm just taking a break!"

Olivia blew out her candles, and everyone asked her what she wished for in the next hundred years.

"I wish the Earth could return to its pristine state," she replied.

Everyone laughed uncertainly, trying to find the humour in her words.

Olivia shook her head. "It's not a joke, I'm a Terrarist now. With an A, not an O."

PART THREE

CAPRIS (LONGER SHORTS)

Sebastian's Sabotage

2051

I don't think he can afford me. Sebastian's heart sank as he walked up the path to the dilapidated door. The uneasiness grew as he noted the small, run-down house, the place at odds with the income listed in Clive's file. *I should have checked the address first before agreeing to take him on.*

After straightening his well-tailored, classically cut suit, he pressed the doorbell and waited. Over the past five years, he'd worked for clients who wanted riches or fame or something else that selfishly made their own life better, and he doubted Clive would be any different. He waited half a minute, then knocked three times on the door. A muffled bang and swearing came from within before the words "I'm coming!" strained through the door. Within seconds, the door opened.

Clive was a slight man, with a forgettable face, thinning blond hair and frown lines on his forehead. His scruffy five o'clock shadow matched the crumpled, stained business attire. Lost for words, Sebastian looked twice at the man who could be mistaken for an older, more dishevelled version of himself in the mirror. The smell of flowers wafted past Clive and into Sebastian's nostrils.

"Clive?" Sebastian asked, then waited for the man to nod. "I'm Sebastian, your two o'clock appointment?"

"I've been expecting you. Please come in." Clive stepped aside, pressing his back against the wall. He held the door open, forcing Sebastian to walk sideways past him into the dim hallway, and the door snicked shut behind him.

"Please excuse the darkness, we're trying a new therapy."

Clive nodded towards the end of the hallway and explained. "Mindfulness."

Sebastian squinted into the darkness, just making out the side of an armchair and its occupant. Clive led him deeper into the house, still speaking low. "Let's go outside. Would you like tea or coffee?"

As Sebastian shook his head, they walked through the neat kitchen and out to the tidy garden. Careful not to offend, Sebastian weighed his words. "You have a... cosy place."

"Hmm, the place. We sold our other one a year ago after I had to take extended unpaid leave to care for Laura. The doctor said she transitioned to menopause early, and she'd always wanted children. The news devastated her, and she's suffered major depression for the last couple of years. I tried my best to make her comfortable, and I've been so focused on her that... well... I couldn't even look after myself," Clive gestured around him.

After the outpouring of too much information, there was a long, awkward pause. Finally, Sebastian broke the silence. "What can I do for you, Clive?"

"I want you to travel back in time to thirty years ago and sabotage Laura's dates for six months until my past self arrives in the city." Clive sighed and furrowed his brow, deepening the marks there. "Her therapist told me she constantly talks about a past relationship from that time, and she never got over it."

Clive wrung his hands. "All Laura focuses on is her therapy instead of living her life with me. I just want her back, and the joy we shared."

"You... realise that's not how it works, right? Once the past changes, this conversation will have never happened," said Sebastian.

"Yes, I know. I just want this reality to end." Clive closed his eyes. "I'm a law-abiding man, but I've tried everything, and I didn't know who else to turn to. We've lost our way, and I can't find a way out. My friend says your work is exceptional."

Sebastian scanned him. In all his experience with altering people's timelines, he'd dealt with greed time and again, but this time it was different. He considered the wreck of a man in front of him, and his morality piqued. Clive's reasons weren't just for himself.

"Do you have an old journal from back then? The entries will guide me onto the right track."

Clive opened his eyes and looked hopefully at him. "You'll take me on?"

Sebastian nodded. "And the payment—"

"I have it ready," Clive interrupted. "I refinanced the house. Hopefully, that will disappear too?"

"It will," Sebastian reassured him. *Then my own life can finally start*, he thought.

2021

Sebastian inhaled a deep breath of the unfamiliar air and coughed a little. He had arrived a week earlier to settle in and find a job to pass the time. Past Clive would move to the city in six months and a week.

The money from this job is all I need to retire, he thought. With his career, his timeline always changed, leaving his relationships untenable. Once he'd returned to his life, and found his girlfriend was no longer his girlfriend; she'd moved on with another man. Similar things had happened to his colleagues. No, he needed to wait until he retired before starting his own family. His mentor had warned Sebastian at the beginning to only stay in this career for five years, or karma would catch up. But six years later, he hadn't been affected physically.

From Laura's journal, he had read how society was opening again after eighteen months in the COVID-19 pandemic. No wonder Laura went a little nuts with dating. The journal showed her dating timeline, listing her dates with various men almost every night, and her varying degrees of success. At the end of the year, she would be steadily dating Tom.

Laura admired the successful man. He'd employed several plumbers in his growing business, and he shared his hopes for a family in the future, but she wasn't ready at the time. Clive had mentioned to Sebastian that for ten years, the couple alternated between wanting and not wanting children. They slowly grew apart and divorced, but the regrets never left her.

When Clive and Laura met after the divorce, they realised they'd lived in the same city for decades. Laura joked in her newer journal that she wished she had met Clive earlier in her life. Maybe they would have had kids together and been happier.

Sebastian had to find a fatal flaw so Laura would shy away from dating Tom. He knew where and when the first date would be, and visited the restaurant several times to scope it out. The large place easily seated a hundred people, with the tables arranged for couples in front of the windows and groups near the bar. The servers wore all black, except for a white bow tie, so it seemed like the perfect spot to blend in.

As the night of the first date drew nearer, Sebastian pored through Laura's journal to find Tom's fatal flaw, ignoring the persistent pang in his stomach. On the third read-through, he found the key: in the middle of their relationship, Laura remarked about how he treated waitstaff, and it wasn't great. Sebastian formulated a plan of attack, then re-read the entry with their first date. After tonight, the journal entry for her first date with Tom would change.

3

He arrived at the restaurant, dressed all in black with a white clip-on bow tie, and signed in for his shift. Just yesterday, he'd had a job interview for a bar position, ferrying drinks to the customers. Without qualifications, serving was the best option to insert himself in the restaurant, and the most efficient way to do his job. The real work would begin when Tom and Laura met at eight p.m., and Sebastian set the alarm on his watch before meeting his supervisor.

When the alarm buzzed a couple of hours later, he looked up just as she walked through the door. Laura was exactly Sebastian's type. She was as bright as her clothing. The little red dress hugged her traditional female curves, and dark blue flats graced her small feet. A mustard-yellow ribbon fluttered over her short black hair as she waited patiently by the podium to be seated.

"Sebastian, wake up! Table ten." His colleague, Dave, rapped his knuckles on the bench-top and pointed to the tray of drinks. Sebastian shifted from where he leant against the bar, gazing dreamily at Laura, his heart thumping. Remembering his mission, he snapped out of it, and the pain in his stomach returned. He hadn't felt a thing while he watched her.

After what seemed like an eternity, the host seated Laura, and Sebastian counted to ten, then poured a glass of icy water. His nerves kicked up the way they always did when he first met his target. He placed the drink on a tray, walked over, and set the glass in front of her as she swiped across the screen of her mobile phone.

"Thank you," she said in a clear voice, without looking up. Sebastian stood there, thinking of something to say. After a few seconds, Laura frowned up at him. "Sorry, do you need something?"

Sebastian lost himself in her cinnamon-coloured eyes for a moment. "Err, yes, would you like a drink?"

"Oh, yes, could I please have a Long Island Iced Tea?" she responded.

"Yes, coming right up." Sebastian turned around as she studied her phone again.

"You've got it bad," Dave muttered after Sebastian gave him her order.

Sebastian shook his head. "She's just another pretty girl, is all..."

"Plenty of pretty girls come here, but she's the first that got you gobsmacked." Dave grinned as he measured the ingredients for Laura's drink. "Just stay awake enough to finish your shift, won't you, dream lover?"

4

Soon after, Tom swaggered in, back ramrod straight with his shoulders pulled back. He waited for the host, who then pointed him towards Laura, where she faced the door, sipping her Long Island Iced Tea, but still scrolling on her phone. Tom squared his already squared shoulders and locked her in his sights. As he approached, Laura looked up and smiled. Tom smiled back in relief.

"Hi," they said together, then laughed nervously.

"Tom?" Laura asked, and he nodded. "I'm Laura, nice to meet you."

"You too, Laura." Tom seated himself at the spare seat, and Sebastian hurried over with a glass of water for the man. Tom ignored him as he stared at Laura, so Sebastian waited until Tom had to acknowledge his presence.

"Yes?"

"Would you like anything to drink?"

"Oh, red wine. Thanks."

"Coming right up." Sebastian walked towards the bar, with one ear tilted towards the couple.

Tom gulped down his glass of water. "Sorry, I'm so thirsty. I've been working all day."

"What do you do?" Laura looked deeply into his eyes.

"I own a plumbing business."

"Oh, I'm sorry," Laura said sympathetically. "I guess you had a tough time during lockdown."

Sebastian tuned out as their small talk continued. He wondered how he would get the job done as he picked up their drinks from Dave and walked back to serve them.

"… responsibility is right. I'm always double-checking that the job is done right, so everyone gets paid. There—"

Tom glanced at Sebastian but didn't spot the trouble heading his way. Sebastian 'accidentally' tripped over his own feet, and the wineglass did a three hundred and sixty degrees somersault before hitting Tom's pristine white shirt. Laura jolted back as some of the splash-back reached her dress. The three of them gaped at Tom's now-red shirt, and the man slowly rose from his chair.

"Look what you've done," Tom growled slowly. He took a few threatening steps towards him until he was well within Sebastian's personal space. "Can you afford to pay me back for this shirt?"

Sebastian stared at him, unmoving.

"No? Well, I'll get my payback." Tom braced Sebastian's pecs and gave a hard shove. Sebastian's arms flailed as he fell back onto the table behind him, food splattering on the customers nearby, before falling to the floor. The whole restaurant hushed as the manager strode out.

"Consider us even." Tom walked back to a slack-jawed Laura and sat back down before pointing at her Long Island Iced Tea. "Are you drinking that?"

Laura couldn't form the words nor make the motions, so Tom reached over for her drink and took several gulps. Finally, she snapped out of it, dug some money from her purse, and put it on the table. "I'm sorry, Tom, I don't think this is gonna work out."

"Enjoy my drink," she said as she escaped.

5

"Are you alright?" Laura crouched beside Sebastian, who watched the exchange from the floor. He nodded as she offered him her hand.

"Yes, I'm fine, thanks." After all these years doing this job, he had a fair idea of how things would go, but not this time. His attraction to Laura clouded his judgement, mixing his present business with his personal future. He had never felt this way about a target, but the brain fog wouldn't lift.

"Come on, let's go outside," she offered, as the restaurant buzz resumed.

The well-lit street was quiet, even more so once the door to the restaurant closed. Out here, the proximity to Laura was more intoxicating. She smelled of jasmine flowers in the springtime.

"Sorry, I won't keep you. I just want to make sure you're okay," Laura said. She asked Sebastian his name, and when he wouldn't respond, she sighed. "I guess you're still in shock."

The door to the restaurant opened, and noise spilled out with Dave. He joined them, his gaze bouncing between the two. "Sebastian, are you alright? You shouldn't have put yourself in that situation; he could have hurt you bad. You look all flushed, let's get you in."

Dave hooked Sebastian's arm over his shoulders and led him inside. As he entered the door, Sebastian looked back and drank in the sight of Laura. Would he see her again?

* * *

6

Sebastian headed back to his tiny apartment, now in two minds about completing the task for Clive. On one hand, he patted himself on the back for thwarting Tom. On the other, he wanted to know more about his knight-ess in shining armour. Sebastian wondered what she was doing now, eager to read about the night's encounter.

After opening the door, he made himself comfortable in his apartment—minimalistic because he didn't think he would stay long enough to decorate. He uncovered Laura's journal from beneath his pillow and settled in for his last night before leaving for 2051. Then he could forget about her; job done.

Sebastian traced Laura's name on the first page, then turned to the last, lazily reading there. But he drifted off as he recalled her cinnamon eyes when she pulled him up off the floor. Then he dreamt about his life after this job. Maybe he could find someone like Laura? He re-read the last page of the journal and bolted upright.

Something was not right.

Instead of a life with Tom, the journal now said she was seeing another guy called Steven, and she was more miserable than before. Sebastian couldn't end the job like this. He talked through his plan with the journal until there was a cross marked against Steven's name, indicating Laura would no longer want to see him.

7

A month later, Sebastian sat in a club, waiting for his date to arrive. Laura hadn't arrived yet, either, nor had her date. The new entries in Laura's journal still concerned him. A year into the future, she would be with Steven. The promiscuous man seemed the sort to sell a used car to a used car salesman, so he easily convinced Laura to take him back time and time again. That left no opening for Laura to meet Clive.

Soon Laura arrived, punctual as always, for her third date with Steven. She was already smitten, and she would have fewer dates with other people after this. Steven arrived a few minutes later, and he sat beside her at the table. Despite the loud music, or maybe because of it, they spoke into each other's ear, both laughing at what the other was saying.

Sebastian drummed his fingers on the table. *Where is she*, he thought. The minutes ticked by as Steven headed to the bar to buy a couple of drinks, passing Sebastian's table. They glanced at each other and both turned away when they made eye contact.

Steven had a kind countenance, one you could tell your deepest secrets to. He wore a dark green polo shirt, jeans, and grey sneakers. Though he might seem nondescript at first glance, his blazing personality meant he kept women easily. As Steven returned to his and Laura's table with their drinks, Sebastian still waited.

Finally, half an hour late, his flustered date bustled through the door. "Sorry, darling, my baby wouldn't settle. How are you?"

Stella's revealing cream dress matched her stilettos. Not his type, but he'd sought her out after researching Steven's social media. He wasn't sure whether she'd tied up her mousy brown hair in a messy bun on purpose, or if she had forgotten to do her hair in the flurry of settling her baby.

Sebastian inwardly flinched. He used people as a means to an end, but the vivacious woman had responsibilities outside her own. Hoping he wouldn't ruin her life too much, he stood and genuinely kissed her cheek.

"I'm good, thanks." He pulled out the other chair, and she sat in it, fanning her face with her purse. The waiter arrived shortly after with a glass of ice-cold water, and she chugged it down. Small rivulets streamed from the corners of her mouth, onto her chest, then disappeared into her cleavage. Sebastian politely looked away, but the corners of his eyes didn't.

"Ahh, that hit the spot." With her thirst quenched, she turned to Sebastian. "So, what are we having for dinner?"

He handed her a menu, and she flicked through.

"I think I know what I want." She lifted her hand to signal the server, then quickly lowered it again. "Oh, do you know what you want?"

Sebastian nodded, so Stella raised her hand again, and the waiter arrived in seconds. "Could I please have a triple steak burger with fries and salad, and a jug of lemon, lime, and bitters? What about you, Sebastian?"

"...I'll have the same," he said, not as confident as her. When the waiter left, Sebastian said, "Are you sure you can eat all that?"

"I'm breastfeeding, hun, I need to keep my nutrients up. My boyfriend broke up with me three months ago, so I'm a single mum now." Stella dejectedly scanned the room, then perked up. "Oh look! There's a jukebox! Let's dance!"

She stood and clutched Sebastian's hand, dragging him towards the jukebox. After she selected a song, retro dance music blared from the speakers, and she hustled him onto the empty dance floor. "Come on!"

The woman danced like a maniac, while Sebastian stood there, arms stiff, and shuffling his feet from side to side. Then he saw his opening. He pulled Stella into his arms and slowly turned them until they faced the other way, then he shifted back. Stella smiled at Sebastian and looked to see what the reactions of the other patrons were.

Suddenly, she froze, her eyes narrowing as she hissed, "That snake!"

She strode over to where Laura and Steven were laughing at each other's jokes. His joy died when Stella slapped his cheek. "Where have you been!"

She turned to Laura next, grabbing her drink and upending it over her head. The shocked couple watched as Stella stalked away to gather her bag from the table before she stormed out. Sebastian was left standing on the dance floor while the jukebox blared its dance music, and the other patrons continued as if nothing had happened.

Laura looked down at her dress, then at Steven. "Who was that?"

"Umm... my cousin...?" he asked, unsure how to handle the situation he'd created. Laura arched an eyebrow.

"She didn't act like your cousin. Are you cheating on her with me?" When Steven looked away, she huffed. "I'm sorry, I'm not that kind of girl. I can't see you anymore."

With that, she beat a hasty retreat.

8

Sebastian quickly walked back to his apartment, eager to return to 2051 and convinced he'd under-charged for this job. When he quietly shut his door behind him, he aimed straight for the journal and opened it to the bookmarked page. Thankfully, the cross marked against Steven's name remained.

Flicking to the last page, he hoped the new entry would tell him Laura had met Clive. But there was no writing. He skimmed backwards until the journal revealed she would be with another man: Ronald.

According to her early journal entries, the first thing Laura noticed was his grooming. Tailored suit, gelled hair, flawless skin; this was a guy who looked after himself. Ronald was a financial consultant and on the way up the career ladder. Plus, Ronald was the perfect gentleman and always offered to cover dinner, but listened to Laura when she insisted on paying. And he'd waited a few dates before sleeping with her.

One day, Laura was running two hours late for their date because of work and had to cancel. Later that evening, Ronald showed up on her doorstep with flowers, charming Laura more, but it was the beginning of the end.

Sebastian eventually uncovered the truth. He found an entry buried in the middle of the journal from Laura's time in the witness protection program. As it turned out, her charming boyfriend found himself in hot water when his high-profile clients were ousted as underworld figures. *What a nightmare.* Sebastian closed his eyes momentarily before searching for the next fatal flaw.

"If only I could sabotage her relationship with Ronald before it ever happened..."

The writing faded a little. Sebastian got excited and continued to talk to the journal, firming up his idea. "What if I met her in person this month, before the dates become regular? I'll be more involved in her life as a friend, and she won't need to date someone new all the time; she'd be happy single." As he clarified his plan to the journal, the entries faded more until Ronald's name disappeared from the writing past today.

9

Sebastian trudged up the stairs, shifting the weight of the box in his arms. He reached the first floor, then walked towards Laura's door. She lived in a beautiful 1920s art deco block of flats, with dark red bricks and curved balconies. While getting a job as a delivery person at her food co-op had been pretty easy, time was of the essence. He only had two more deliveries before she started dating Ronald.

After gently placing the box of fruit and veg on the floor, he rang her doorbell. He focused on the food at his feet until the door opened.

"Hi Sebastian," Laura sang the words to a tune. She retraced her steps inside as Sebastian picked up the box and followed her. Gesturing at her counter, she sat on the couch. She was extremely chatty the previous week, not letting him go for an hour, and she hadn't recognised his forgettable face from their past disastrous encounters.

"Do you like Sia?" Laura asked him.

"I don't listen to music..." Sebastian murmured.

"Oh, you're weird..." Laura winced. "Sorry, I didn't mean to say that. My mouth has its own mind sometimes."

"It's okay, my friends made fun of me all the time because of it."

Laura thought. "Maybe you haven't heard anything you like yet. I like easy listening radio stations; they often have a variety of things over several decades on there." She stretched over to her phone on the side table and flicked her finger on the screen. Soft strains of sixty-year-old music began playing over the Bluetooth speakers, which gradually got louder until it reached Laura's desired volume.

Sebastian frowned as he gradually recognised Joni Mitchell's 'Big Yellow Taxi'.

"What's wrong?" Laura asked.

Sebastian shook his head. "My ex loved this song. It's a classic."

"Your ex?!" Laura suddenly seemed interested.

"Yeah. I wanted kids, and she said I didn't spend enough time with her to have kids. So, we broke up."

Laura looked away. "I can see where she's coming from. You need to spend time with your kids to raise them. That's why I don't want kids right now, but I do in the future."

Sebastian was thoughtful. "I intended to be there for them, she just couldn't wait until I made enough..."

"And I can see where you're coming from. I feel the same," Laura replied.

The song ended, so Sebastian changed the subject. "Anyway, I hate this song. If anything, I like classical pop."

Laura tilted her head. "Classical pop. I've never heard that one before. Do you have a playlist?"

Sebastian paused, then shook his head. "You might know some of them: Madonna, ABBA, Olivia Newton-John."

"Oh, yeah, those are old enough to be classics." She laughed. "Here, I have a playlist. I'll put it on for you."

Laura flicked again at her phone screen, and Michael Jackson blared from the speakers. She left her seat to dance on the beige rug between her sofa and the TV, and raised her voice over the music. "Come on!"

Sebastian's toe-tapping ceased as he shook his head and crossed his arms. "I can't, sorry."

"What do you mean?" she stopped dancing. "You don't have a medical condition, do you?"

"I can't dance, does that count?"

"Oh, everyone can dance." Laura beamed, and she skipped around the sofa towards him in time with the beat, holding out her hands and shimmying her shoulders. "Even you!"

He froze. "No. I can't dance. You can't make me."

"Is it because you're self-conscious? Just close your eyes and pretend you're the only one here."

"Alright, I'll try. But I'm warning you, you'll regret it." He closed his eyes and moved away from the counter, sighing. "I'm a bad dancer."

His first small movements were more like twitches until Laura grabbed his hands and waved them around, commanding him to move! So, he moved his shoulders to one beat, and his legs to another.

"I like this!" he said loudly, as his head and torso joined in two other beats. When the song ended, Sebastian opened his eyes. Laura's body was still, eyes wide, mouth ajar, and he smiled at her. "How'd I go?"

Laura rocked on her heels before she walked around him. "Err, you did fine. Want a glass of water? You must be thirsty."

Sebastian waited for her praise as she rounded the counter to the fridge, bent, and hid behind the door. When the realisation hit him that she wouldn't, his face flushed, and a bead of sweat dripped down his temple. "Sorry, gotta go."

10

Back at the apartment, Sebastian leant back on the closed

door. He couldn't believe he had made a fool of himself in front of her, of all people, the one he needed to impress the most. He took a cursory glance at Laura's journal on the counter, looked away as he didn't want to see what she wrote there about him, then walked over to his bed and flopped face down.

"Aaaahhhh," he screamed into his pillow. The embarrassment branded his face, and he could still feel the tingle on his arms where her hands had held them. He thought he was pretty good with girls, but when he reached a certain threshold of like, he did ridiculous things. Now there were danger signs flashing around his client's future wife, and he still had a few months before Clive arrived.

There was a knock on the door, and Sebastian frowned. He didn't know anyone here, but he walked over to the door and squinted through the peephole. It was Laura. And she was holding a glass of water.

His heart leapt, then his face flushed. He struggled to compose himself enough for a sensible response, but shouted through the door instead. "What do you want?"

"I just thought you wanted a glass of water, and you left before you could have some," came the muffled reply.

"How do you know where I live? That's really creepy."

"I followed you."

Sebastian swore under his breath. Did he walk that slowly? He peered through the peephole again. Laura looked straight at him, and he flinched away. "Sorry, Laura, I'm really busy, so I can't stay to talk. I'll see you next week."

"You can see me earlier if you like, and you know where I live. Come by on Tuesday. I'll make you lunch." She crouched to put something on the floor, then left.

When Sebastian was sure she had left, he opened the door a crack and found the glass of water, which he presumed she had carried all the way from her place. When he picked it up, a piece of paper floated down. Upon landing, a hand-drawn smiley face teased him.

* * *

11

Dave dried a glass throughout Sebastian's deafening silence until it was too much, then he threw out a wild guess. "She's not worth it, mate."

"I know." Sebastian released the breath he didn't know he was holding. "I just want to finish this job, go home, and start a family."

"Do you have a girl waiting for you back home?" Dave asked.

"No, I couldn't while I was working. Things kept changing while I was gone..."

"Are you hoping Laura will be that girl?"

Sebastian paused for a long while. *Do I?* he thought as he stared into his glass of whiskey. "No, she's taken."

"There are plenty of goannas in the outback."

"Not until I finish this job, though."

12

The next four months flew by, thanks to Laura's easy company. Since nothing bad had happened to Sebastian yet, he figured he'd held the karma at bay. He checked the journal about once a month to make sure the plan stayed on track. The final entry was Clive and Laura's first Valentine's Day together in six months.

One day, they ambled down a wide, tree-lined avenue in the city, when Laura grabbed his elbow and pointed someone out. "Look, Seb, it's your doppelgänger!"

Sebastian followed the squealing woman's finger and spotted the man with the same hair, same-coloured clothes, same build. But the mannerisms were all wrong. *Clive's here.* The job would soon be over, and Sebastian's heart leapt at the thought.

"Let's go over and take a photo!" Laura dragged Sebastian over to Clive. She squealed again before bombarding Clive. "Sorry to bother you, could we please take a photo with you? You and Seb look exactly alike! What's your name? Are you a twin?"

"Err... Clive. I'm an only child as far as I know."

Laura dragged Sebastian next to Clive and took photos with her phone, while Sebastian shook the oblivious man's hand. He'd expected that. "Nice to meet you, Clive."

"I just moved here from Perth for work. I don't know anyone here," said Clive. He happily followed Laura's directions for them to move their arms up and down in sync.

Sebastian's heart tugged. He'd have to leave Laura's joyful world, but he had to complete his work. With a half-hearted smile, he nodded at Clive. "Great, you can hang with us if you want."

Laura returned to show them the photos on her phone. "See, you look exactly the same!"

Clive laughed. "There's no denying it... what's your name again?"

"Laura," she said as they shook hands.

Sebastian stepped aside. "I'll just grab a drink of water."

"OK, go get your drink." Laura and Clive's laughter mingled as she dismissed Sebastian with a wave.

Heavy, he trudged to the bubbler.

13

Another week passed, with Laura and Sebastian showing Clive around the city in their spare time. When Sebastian arrived at work, he nodded to Dave gravely, and his friend frowned. "You look like you need a drink. What's up, mate?"

"Nothing..."

"Aww, come on, you can tell your ol' friend Dave."

Dave was a great listener, and Sebastian had come close to

telling him everything so many times. He shook his head, though.

"Okay, well, I'm here when you need me."

There was no denying the attraction between Clive and Laura, and the journal confirmed it. Despite the glaring truth, Sebastian couldn't handle watching them fall in love, so he took on extra shifts at the restaurant where he and Laura first met.

A few times, he had considered pretending he'd never taken on the job. No one else in the world knew about his work... but he couldn't bear to think about lying to himself. There was a limit to the questionable things he would do.

Lately, his stomach pain had returned. *Maybe karma has caught up with me?* Being in his sixth year on the job, he was long overdue to retire. But he couldn't just leave the job, especially when he needed the money. *Maybe I can just take the money and go? I've been here long enough; I think I've earned it.*

Just the thought of failing Clive and now Laura worsened his stomach pangs a million times, and he doubled over as if he'd been punched in the gut. His head spun, then everything went black.

14

Dave stepped into the hospital room, rustling a bag of snacks as he sat in the visitor's chair, while Sebastian lay on the uncomfortable bed, facing the window. He didn't feel well enough to watch the TV above the bed, so he stared at the brick wall of the building opposite. Dave scrolled through his social media, watching videos of dogs and cats being themselves and chuckling to himself every so often.

"Dave, you don't need to be here," Sebastian murmured. Whatever was wrong had drained him, and even though he hated bothering Dave, the company relieved him.

Dave chuckled again at the video on his phone. "It's okay, it's my day off."

The doctor had done their rounds earlier while Dave visited the kiosk. She seemed kind enough, but he didn't understand a word she said. Too much antiquated jargon, so the only words he recognised were scans and brain. He continued staring out the window.

"Do you have family here?" Dave asked, and when Sebastian shook his head, he sighed. "Just wondering who we should inform that you're in the hospital. The doctor—"

"The doctor knows nothing," Sebastian interrupted tightly. He didn't want to be here anymore, but he felt too weak to leave the bed, and he needed his strength to return to his own time. Really, his job here was done.

Was this karma's way of getting back at him?

"What about that girl you're seeing?"

"She's just a friend." Sebastian curled into the foetal position as the painful reality cramped his stomach.

"You 'right, mate?" Dave pocketed his phone and reached through the monitors to place a hand on Sebastian's shoulder. He found the call-button and pressed it.

The nurse came after five minutes of Dave's restless pacing. "He's in a lot of pain. You got anything?"

The nurse scanned Sebastian's face, then the monitors, answering as she walked out. "I'll let the doctor know."

Dave's hand remained on Sebastian's shoulder, softly patting him.

2051

Sebastian left 2021 without a word to anyone, not even Dave. After the doctors found nothing physically wrong with him, they discharged him from the hospital with anti-anxiety meds in his pocket. He didn't quite believe the doctor's diagnosis, but the pills *did* keep the stomach pangs at bay. Before leaving, he had taken one last look at Laura's journal to check she was still with Clive, then burned it.

Now, their address was in a nicer neighbourhood.

Still wearing the same crumpled clothes he'd worn to the hospital, Sebastian walked towards their house in 2051. They shouldn't recognise him after his week of extreme weight loss in hospital and thirty years' distance, plus the make-up he applied to look extra gaunt. His stomach cramped, and he swallowed a pill.

Meddling with other people's lives usually ended badly for his colleagues, and Sebastian had considered himself one of the lucky ones. Karma finally caught up with him, though. *Was the pain worth his need to retire by thirty?* He couldn't be sure, but for now he needed to check the couple were fine for his own peace of mind, and then he could go home.

The federation-style house in the quiet street was well-maintained, and the freshly clipped grass in the front yard, sweetened the air. He strode up the footpath and rang the bell, and the door opened to a man in his twenties.

The younger version of Clive greeted him. "Hello, can I help you?"

"Hi, I have a two o'clock with Clive? I'm Taylor." Sebastian had rehearsed for this moment, to use the least amount of energy possible.

"Sure, hang on a sec. Dad!" the young man called out and turned, waving Sebastian inside. "He'll be out soon, come in."

Sebastian closed the door behind him and followed him along the neat hallway. Formal and informal family photos filled the walls, and Sebastian longed to study the evidence of a happy life. The young man guided Sebastian to a small room at the back of the house, with a desk and two chairs on either side. Clive's office.

After settling in a seat, he waited a short while until a man stepped through the door. Clive wasn't the slight, untidy man from before. He wore a smart-casual polo shirt and jeans, and laugh lines bracketed his mouth.

As Clive sat at his desk opposite Sebastian, he greeted him

with a friendly smile before squinting. "You know, you look just like a guy—"

Laura knocked on the door. "Hi honey, would your guest like a drink?"

Sebastian turned his head sideways to hide his face but viewed her in his peripheral vision. She was plumper than the last time he saw her in 2021, but healthy, and she carried a glass of water. His insides twisted as he nodded, and he reached for the pill bottle in his pocket. Laura set the glass in front of him and left.

"What can I do for you, Taylor?" Clive asked as Sebastian clutched the pill bottle.

"My aunt is quite frail, so I'm looking for a registered nurse," Sebastian said. Distracted, his shaky fingers fiddled with the bottle top. "I'm just interviewing a few people at this stage."

Clive looked away for privacy as Sebastian took a pill. "You've come to the right place. We have several registered nurses on our books."

They discussed options for Sebastian's fictional aunt, and Clive impressed him. This guy had it all together now. Not the wrecked human being from their first meeting. Sebastian rose from his seat. "Thank you, that's all I need for now. I'll let you know."

"Great, thanks, Taylor. All the best with your aunt." Clive walked Sebastian to the door.

"Thanks, and all the best to you too. You have a beautiful family," Sebastian said as he faced Clive.

"Yes, thank you. We're comfortable and happy." Clive looked Sebastian up and down. "But first, you should take care of yourself before looking after others."

"If you have the capacity..." Sebastian grimaced for a microsecond, then smiled. "Seems like you do, though."

Clive smiled back before they shook hands, and he shut the door quietly on Sebastian. The couple's grandchildren squealed and laughed in the backyard, their joy drifting in the air, and he regretfully concluded that his job was done well.

No more, no less.
What a way for karma to end my career.

63

One Last Adventure

The schoolkids moved on to the next museum display, leaving Roo intrigued. The museum curator had commented about treasures waiting through the closed door behind her, so Roo hung back from the group. Her best friend, Sue, stuck with her as always while they waited for everyone's attention to shift away from them.

When they were alone, she opened the door, and the pair snuck into the mystery room, quickly closing the door behind them once they were inside. The lights down the corridor flashed on in sequence, the furthest ones turning on a few seconds after the ones above their heads.

"See, told you it was a good idea!" Roo said.

Sue scrunched her nose. "There's nothing interesting here. Just old boxes of stuff."

"Come on, Sue. Look." Roo searched the room for something, *anything*, to make their last adventure memorable. She toed the lid off a box close to the door, and a dim, pulsing blue light beckoned.

"Susy! Ruby!" The muffled voice of their teacher called from the outer room.

Time was running out, so Roo reached into the box,

grabbed the pulsing watch lying on top, and tucked it inside her pocket.

2

Professor Alan Staedfast carefully balanced his morning cup of coffee with one hand as he navigated through the maze of corridors in Australia's Commonwealth Scientific and Industrial Research Organisation (CSIRO). Having burnt out at his academic job, he took a secondment to the Donations Division in the Melbourne offices. His boss called it a 'vacation job', and so far, she had been right: everything of note had happened in the past.

Staedfast arrived at his make-shift office and settled in to sort through the next box of items that had belonged to Dr Childers. The man had passed five years prior, and his professional effects arrived just yesterday as part of the estate settlement. He ignored the handover sheet and cut through the taped lid to open the box.

A pulsing blue light beckoned from within.

3

After the excursion, Sue invited Roo back to her place. They edged past the moving boxes filling the hallway, and into Sue's almost empty bedroom. Patchy, the family dog, bounded up to Sue and Roo with her tail wagging in a wide arc.

"Sue, Roo! You're home!" Patchy exclaimed through her DNA-enabled neural lace, and Sue crouched and rubbed Patchy's rump.

"Yes, Patchy, good girl," she crooned as the dog's tongue lolled in pleasure.

Next week, Sue and her family would move to the other side of the Australian continent. The two hadn't really discussed it. Sue had never moved house and didn't worry too much, but Roo didn't like the thought of being left behind.

Her young heart hurt as she skimmed the boxes full of Sue's stuff. She had moved house so many times, and her mum promised they'd stay for good this time. It had felt safe to make a real friend.

They shut themselves in Sue's room, and Roo took the treasure from her pocket. Sue peered into her best friend's hands, where the fifty-year-old watch continued to pulse blue light. It was an old smartwatch from fifty years ago. Roo's Nana had shown her a similar one and told her how the Singularity made wearable devices obsolete. Roo turned it over in her hands.

Sue poked at it. "How does it work?"

"Just put it on your wrist. Like this." Roo circled the band around Sue's wrist and adjusted the strap.

The pulsing blue light stopped, and the word 'Emergency' appeared on the screen. They looked up at each other.

"Press it. Can always undo it later," Roo said.

"Dunno... maybe—" Sue began, but Roo had already pressed the button.

4

As Staedfast laid out and examined the other items from Dr Childer's estate, the building's emergency systems triggered his neural lace. False alarms occurred often, so he and his few office mates calmly filed out to meet the other teams at the emergency meeting point. His supervisor hurried down the hallway, though. Aiming straight for him.

"What do you have there?" he asked Staedfast, pointing at the old smartwatch on his wrist.

"A watch from Childer's box of inventions. It flashed blue

until I put it on, then I forgot about it."

"It's not flashing blue now. Look, it says 'Emergency'."

Staedfast twisted the watch face towards him, shading it with his hand as he squinted at the bright light.

5

Sue and Roo goggled as a waveform appeared on the watch face.

"Welcome, Dr Devhi," a husky male voice from the watch said. "What would you like to do next? Call Dr Childers, or stop emergency?"

The girls glanced at each other. Sue yelled, "Stop emergency," while Roo shouted, "Call Dr Childers."

The watch's voice responded. "Did you say escalate the emergency? Initiating the sequence in five... four..."

6

The augmented reality in the neural lace of the workers from the surrounding buildings, continued the insistent alarm as they waited outside. A colleague nudged Staedfast. "What do you think? Should we press it?"

Staedfast shrugged. "There's no harm in it, it's a fifty-year-old watch."

When he pressed the button on the watch face, the alarms blared louder, and they covered their ears, even though the alarms came from their neural lace. His colleague looked him in the eyes and pursed his lips in a Filipino-style gesture at something over Staedfast's shoulder.

He turned around. People at the meeting point scattered in all directions, while he tracked the feathered shape of a giant T-Rex, from its feet to its teeth. It shimmered in the bright sun, but then the image jittered as it shifted forward.

"It's a hologram!" Staedfast yelled over and over, waving his arms at the panicking crowd.

7

Sue pointed out the window. A gigantic, feathered foot rested outside, and Roo's eyes widened. She slowly pressed the watch face on Sue's wrist. When the feathered foot disappeared, Sue's eyes widened as well.

8

Staedfast and his colleague looked around. Their feathered friend was gone, too. They glanced at the watch face, and a telephone icon with the name 'Dr Devhi' had replaced the emergency label.

9

Sue's neural lace alerted her to an incoming call from an unknown number. Her fathers had set call filters so only trusted sources could contact her. She answered without a second thought.

"Dr Devhi?"

"Hello, who is this?" Sue asked, staring at Roo.

"Who is this?"

"This is Sue, who are you?"

"This is Professor Alan Staedfast, from the CSIRO. Can I speak to Dr Devhi, please?"

* * *

10

Staedfast focused on the smartwatch while he waited for the reply. Production had ceased long ago, but some of the functionality must link to the neural lace. He wasn't sure how it was possible, as the factory setting of the last smartwatches was separate from the neural lace system, and only interfaced with it.

"Hello, it's Dr Devhi." It had to be a child imitating a deep voice.

11

Roo listened in on the call through Sue's neural lace via her home Wi-Fi. When Sue muted her phone, they discussed what might happen if they were grounded for her last week here. But they couldn't pass up the opportunity of meeting someone from the CSIRO, the famous Australian research organisation.

"Dr Devhi, there has been an emergency here. Is everything okay on your end?" Staedfast asked.

"No, we saw a dinosaur foot outside my window. It's gone now." Sue's voice quivered, and Roo glared at her.

"Interesting, same here. Where are you located?"

The neural lace popped up the location of Sue's house, and they shared it with Staedfast.

"Oh, you're in Sydney, I'm in Melbourne. I'll take the train up tomorrow and meet you."

"But we'll be in sch—" Sue almost gave them away, but Roo pushed her.

Roo answered in her deepest voice. "We'll be there."

* * *

12

Staedfast caught the fast train from Melbourne to Sydney, the trip taking three hours of his morning. *I will be back home for dinner,* he thought. While he rode the train, the dinosaur appeared briefly outside again. None of the train passengers seemed fussed, though, they thought it was another train advertisement.

He changed trains and boarded one heading to Ashfield, a suburb in the inner west of Sydney. When the quick trip ended, he walked the rest of the way, passing several multi-level apartment buildings not far from the train line, which eventually gave way to single-level houses. He stopped to face a white house with brown trimmings and a moving truck in the driveway. The map in the neural lace told him he was here. He considered the best way to retrieve Dr Devhi's long-lost watch and bring the two last smartwatches together.

13

Sue and Roo waited at the front window, still celebrating how easily they'd escaped school. The girls attended in the morning but pressed the emergency button on the smartwatch at recess. As the feathered dinosaur stomped around, the kids fled in terror, and the principal declared through the neural lace that the school would close for the rest of the day. They'd walked calmly out the gates just as the authorities arrived to investigate.

They watched as Staedfast hesitated in front of Sue's house and just stood there.

"What's he waiting for?" Roo whispered.

Patchy walked past, stopping to growl when she saw what they were looking at. "There's an intruder outside; he's acting funny."

***

14

Staedfast checked the smartwatch on his wrist. He hadn't expected that working in the Donations Division would lead to an adventure, but it had. Now, he wondered how Childers and Devhi resisted the Singularity for their whole lives, as it was so entrenched in humanity's DNA now, and the neural lace's reach extended throughout his body.

15

Sue and Roo couldn't wait any longer, so they ran outside to greet Staedfast. After clearing up who was who, Staedfast got down to business, and thankfully, Patchy ended her growling.

"Dr Devhi, whose watch you have now, invented many things. But not many people use them now because most of her inventions used the smartwatch. Same for Dr Childers. Apart from creating holograms of dinosaurs within the augmented reality of any neural lace nearby, something amazing happens once the two watches are together. Do you have Dr Devhi's watch?"

Sue and Roo nodded. When Roo removed the watch from her pocket, Staedfast took Childer's one out of his man bag.

"Please put it on," he instructed, putting Childer's watch on himself.

As soon as Roo did, a shimmering sphere enclosed Staedfast and Roo.

"Now, no one can hear us, Roo. Not even Sue or Patchy. The watch creates a sphere of silence and locks out anyone outside the sphere."

On the other side of the bubble, Sue shouted, "What are you saying? I can't hear you!"

Patchy cocked her head as Roo nodded quickly and took off Devhi's watch. The sphere disappeared. While Roo explained, Sue worried. She needed to bring her friend down to Earth, not gain a way to plan more shenanigans.

"Now, did you know Dr Devhi in any way? She lived close to here."

Roo elbowed Sue so she couldn't respond before her.

"It's in a box of stuff," she said, omitting the actual location.

"Where was this box?" Staedfast pressed.

Sue put her hand over Roo's mouth. "In the museum."

She preferred to tell the truth, while a disgruntled Roo licked her hand. "Eww!"

"That explains it. Dr Devhi's watch has been missing for several years," he said with a glint in his eye. "You know, you don't need these smartwatches for a sphere of silence. I can give you the program, but only in exchange for the watch. I should warn you, though, anything you say is recorded as potential evidence in case you commit a crime."

The girls narrowed their eyes. They knew how switcheroo tricks worked, they'd done it themselves. There was that instance when everyone at school brought in trading cards, and when a rare one appeared, Roo used a magic trick her mum had taught her to make it disappear.

"Can we test it?" Roo asked.

"Of course. I'll upload the program when you're ready."

They whispered amongst themselves for a bit, then Sue raced inside to tell her daddy that she'd call for him in a few moments. Shortly, she returned and nodded to Staedfast.

He uploaded the program to both of their accounts.

Roo and Sue accessed their neural lace and activated the program, then the sphere appeared around them. As a test, Sue screamed for her daddy, who was inside the house, and waited for him to appear. When he didn't, Roo and Sue jumped on the spot and hugged each other.

Staedfast smiled as the sphere disappeared. "The five-dimensional sphere works no matter how far you are. Not only can you talk to each other, but you can see, hear, and feel anything that the other is experiencing. As long as you're connected to the cloud, it will work. Are you happy with it?"

They nodded enthusiastically, and Patchy, caught up in the excitement, said, "Yes, yes, yes!"

"Are you ready to give me the watch?" Staedfast held out his hand and Roo handed him Dr Devhi's watch.

16

Staedfast arrived back at his Melbourne home after the fruitful day. While the watches were useless in this day and age and belonged in a museum, giving the two girls a way to connect once they separated, satisfied him. He sat at his computer to write his report, eagerly inserting the right keywords as evidence for his next promotion.

17

Roo and Sue stood in the driveway as Sue's dads packed the final bags into the car. The truck had already left the empty house behind. Roo gave Sue a big hug.

"I'll miss you." A few gentle tears streaked down her cheeks, and Roo quickly wiped them away before her best friend could see. Sue hugged her back, hard.

"Yeah..." she never really knew what to say about her moving away. She still didn't. But she was glad—

Roo completed her thought in a whisper. "Glad we had our last adventure together."

Patchy looked up at them, tail thumping against the car. She crooned and softly agreed.

Motifs

- The Loyal Key: *Objects, Coming home, Loyalty.*
- The Filthy Tea Towel: *Intergenerational, Objects, Memories.*
- Freedom: *Objects, Transformation, Shapeshifter.*
- New Branch: *Family, Time travel.*
- Storm: *Dog, Shifting fortunes, Loyalty.*
- Hierarchical Ambition: *Career scientist, Loyalty, Poker-face.*
- No Longer Brave: *Haircut, Confidence.*

- TherA: *AI, Therapist, Schizophrenia.*
- Digital Air: *Curing pain, Future Earth.*
- What Was Lost: *Dingo, Fear, Shifting Fortunes.*
- Terrarist: *Climate change, Terraforming, Future Earth, Time Dilation.*

- Sebastian's Sabotage: *Time travel, Shifting fortunes.*
- One Last Adventure: *Neural lace, Museum, Future Earth, Dog.*

What did you think of Broad Shorts? Please leave a review at:
a-whim-away.com.au/review?
utm_source=Broad+Shorts+Book&utm_medium=D
irect&utm_campaign=referral&utm_id=Referral

Please recommend Broad Shorts to your
friends!
a-whim-away.com.au/broad-shorts?
utm_source=Broad+Shorts+Book&utm_medium=D
irect&utm_campaign=referral&utm_id=Referral

Thanks for stopping by!

www.ingramcontent.com/pod-product-compliance
Lightning Source LLC
Chambersburg PA
CBHW051005050726
47592CB00007B/2713